It's Mine!

It's Mine!

by Leo Lionni

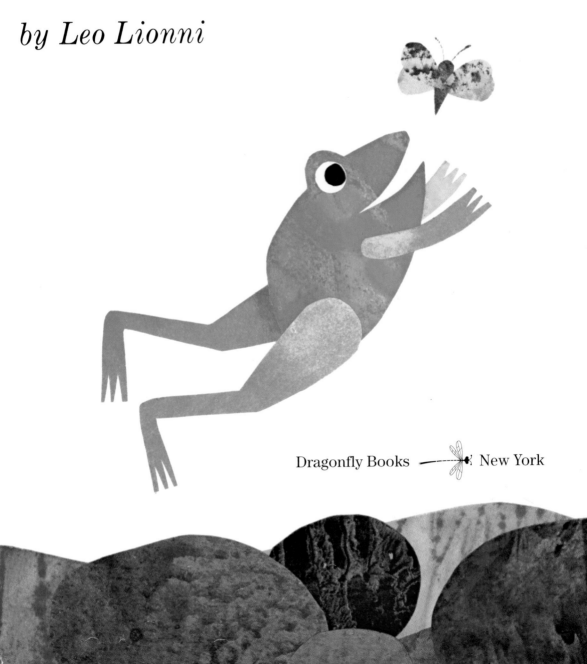

Dragonfly Books ⟶ New York

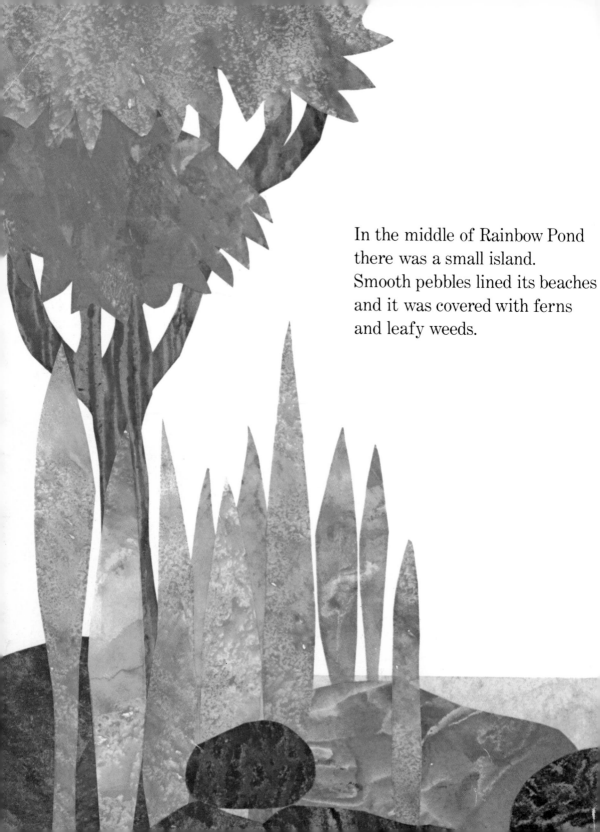

In the middle of Rainbow Pond
there was a small island.
Smooth pebbles lined its beaches
and it was covered with ferns
and leafy weeds.

On the island lived three quarrelsome frogs named Milton, Rupert, and Lydia. They quarreled and quibbled from dawn to dusk.

"Stay out of the pond!" yelled Milton. "The water is mine."

"Get off the island!" shouted Rupert. "The earth is mine."

"The air is mine!" screamed Lydia as she leaped
to catch a butterfly. And so it went.

One day a large toad appeared before them.

"I live on the other side of the island," he said, "but I can hear you shouting 'It's mine! It's mine! It's mine!' all day long. There is no peace because of your endless bickering. You can't go on like this!" With that the toad slowly turned around and hopped away through the weeds.

No sooner had he left than Milton ran off with a large worm. The others hopped after him. "Worms are for everybody!" they cried.

But Milton croaked defiantly, "Not this one. It's mine!"

Suddenly the sky darkened and a rumble
of distant thunder circled the island.
Rain filled the air, and the water turned to
mud. The island grew smaller and smaller
as it was swallowed up by the rising
flood. The frogs were scared.

Desperately they clung to the few
slippery stones that still rose above the
wild, dark water. But soon these too
began to disappear.

There was only one rock left and there the frogs huddled, trembling from cold and fright. But they felt better now that they were together, sharing the same fears and hopes. Little by little the flood subsided. The rain fell gently and then stopped altogether.

But look! The large rock that had saved them was no rock at all.
"You saved us!" shouted the frogs when they recognized the toad.

The next morning the water had cleared. Sunrays
chased silver minnows on the sandy bottom of the pond.
Joyfully the frogs jumped in, and side by side
they swam all around the island.

Together they leaped after the swarms of butterflies that filled the air.

And later, when they rested in the weeds, they felt happy
in a way they had never been before.

"Isn't it peaceful," said Milton.
"And isn't it beautiful," said Rupert.
"And do you know what else?" said Lydia.
"No, what?" the others asked.
"It's ours!" she said.

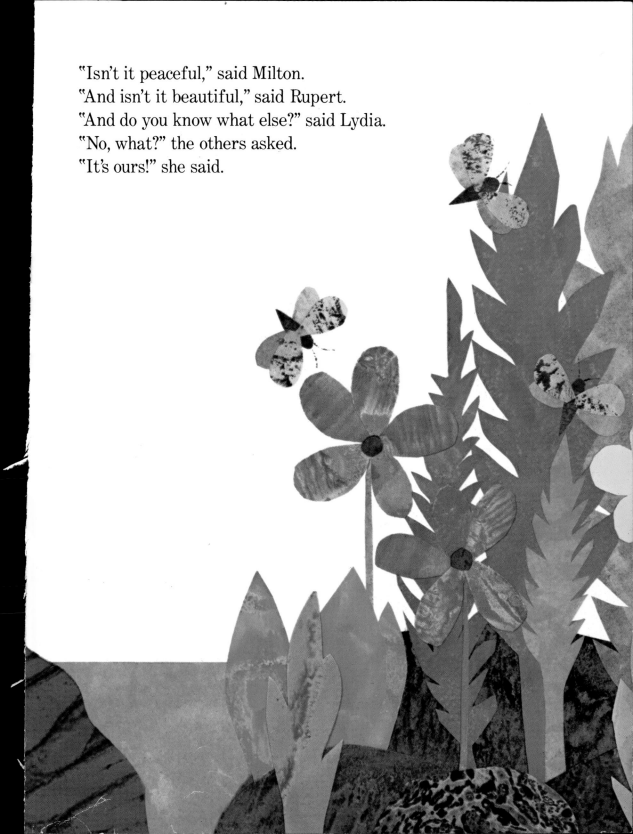

About the Author

Leo Lionni, an internationally known designer, illustrator, and graphic artist, was born in Holland and studied in Italy until he came to the United States in 1939. He was the recipient of the 1984 American Institute of Graphic Arts Gold Medal and was honored posthumously in 2007 with the Society of Illustrators Lifetime Achievement Award. His picture books are distinguished by their enduring moral themes, graphic simplicity, and brilliant use of collage, and include four Caldecott Honor Books: *Inch by Inch, Frederick, Swimmy*, and *Alexander and the Wind-Up Mouse*. Hailed as "a master of the simple fable" by the *Chicago Tribune*, he died in 1999 at the age of 89.

Copyright © 1985, 1986 by Leo Lionni

All rights reserved. Published in the United States by Dragonfly Books, an imprint of Random House Children's Books, a division of Random House, Inc., New York. Originally published in hardcover in the United States by Alfred A. Knopf, an imprint of Random House Children's Books, a division of Random House, Inc., New York, in 1986.

Dragonfly Books with the colophon is a registered trademark of Random House, Inc.

Visit us on the Web! www.randomhouse.com/kids

Educators and librarians, for a variety of teaching tools, visit us at www.randomhouse.com/teachers

Library of Congress Cataloging-in-Publication Data

Lionni, Leo. It's mine!
Summary: Three selfish frogs quarrel over who owns their pond and island, until a storm makes them value the benefits of sharing.
ISBN: 978-0-394-87000-7 (trade) — ISBN: 978-0-394-97000-4 (lib. bdg.) — ISBN: 978-0-679-88084-4 (pbk.)
1. Children's stories, American. [1. Selfishness—Fiction. 2. Sharing—Fiction. 3. Frogs—Fiction.]
I. Title. II. Title: It's mine!   PZ7.L6634It 1986   [E] 85000190

MANUFACTURED IN CHINA

28 27 26 25 24 23